KU-711-624

# Peter
## puts his
# foot
## in it!

RO WILLOUGHBY

ILLUSTRATED BY
JOEL BUCKLEY

Copyright © Ro Willoughby 2004
First published 2004
ISBN 1 85999 765 1

Scripture Union, 207-209 Queensway, Bletchley, Milton Keynes,
MK2 2EB, England.
Email: info@scriptureunion.org.uk
Website: www.scriptureunion.org.uk

Scripture Union Australia, Locked Bag 2, Central Coast Business Centre,
NSW 2252
Website: www.su.org.au

Scripture Union USA, PO Box 987, Valley Forge, PA 19482
Website: www.scriptureunion.org

All rights reserved. No part of this publication may be reproduced, stored in a
retrieval system, or transmitted in any form or by any means, electronic, mechanical,
photocopying, recording or otherwise, without the prior permission of Scripture
Union.

The right of Ro Willoughby to be identified as author of this work has been asserted
by her in accordance with the Copyright, Designs and Patents Act 1988.

Joel Buckley has asserted his right under the Copyright, Designs and Patents Act 1988,
to be identified as illustrator of this work.

British Library Cataloguing-in-Publication Data.

A catalogue record of this book is available from the British Library.

Printed and bound in Great Britain by Creative Print and Design (Wales) Ebbw Vale.

Cover design: kwgraphicdesign

Scripture Union is an international Christian charity working with
churches in more than 130 countries, providing resources to bring the good
news about Jesus Christ to children, young people and families and to encourage
them to develop spiritually through the Bible and prayer.

As well as our network of volunteers, staff and associates who run holidays,
church-based events and school Christian groups, we produce a wide range of
publications and support those who use our resources through training
programmes.

# CONTENTS

SPECIAL THANKS TO MY FRIEND, NAOMI KING, AGED 10, FOR HER WISE ADVICE. R.W

FOR NIKKI. J.B.

# WHO'S WHO?

**Peter:** This book is all about him. He was a fisherman, and ran his family's fishing business on Lake Galilee, with Andrew, his brother. He was known as Simon until his friend Jesus gave him a new name, Peter, which means 'Rock'.

**Andrew:** He was Peter's brother, and also a fisherman. He met Jesus before Peter did, and introduced them to each other.

**John:** He ran another family fishing business on the lake, and worked with his brother, James. His father was called Zebedee. (Say it "Zeb-Ed-eee"!) Both James and John were friends of Jesus too.

**Jesus:** He grew up in Nazareth, which was a town near Lake Galilee. He worked there as a carpenter. When he was 30 years old, he began telling people about how God wanted them to live. He travelled around, meeting people, talking with them, healing and caring for them. He invited 12 men to be his close friends and travel with him. They were called 'disciples'. Peter, Andrew, John and James were four of these friends.

To get the best out of *Peter puts his foot in it!*, begin at the beginning!

CHAPTER 1

# NAME CHANGE!

Simon was tired…
he had been on
his feet all night.
When he was
working in his
fishing boat, his
feet were never
still!

Simon looked across at his brother, Andrew, who was pulling huge, tough nets out of their boat. Last night had been a good night.

They worked with two other brothers called James and John. On a good night, the four of them caught lots of fish in their two boats, and sold them in the market the next morning. You can guess how many fish they caught on a bad night!

LOOK AT ALL THESE NEW HOLES IN THE NET, ANDREW. IT'LL TAKE AGES TO MEND THEM!

All morning, Simon sat mending the nets and talking with anyone who came by. Andrew had to listen to him most of the time. At last, every torn bit of netting was mended.

I'M GOING HOME, ANDREW.

But Andrew had gone – he was nowhere to be seen. He hadn't even bothered to say "Goodbye!" Simon frowned. His tummy rumbled.

Simon's wife was a very good cook. She gave Simon a huge, warm bread roll for lunch which smelt wonderful and tasted delicious.

MmMMM!

Simon licked his lips and sighed. He went outside to have a rest in the warm sunshine and soon…

Andrew, unlike his brother, didn't go home for lunch. He had something important to do. A few weeks ago a strange man call John came into the village nearby. John was a wild man who lived out in the fields and spent all his time talking with people. Andrew loved to listen to him. He talked about God and how God wanted people to live. He talked about a man who was coming soon who came from God.

This man was called 'Messiah'! (Say it quickly – "Ms I R".)

That afternoon, Andrew went into the country to talk with John. He had lots of questions to ask him and John had lots of answers! Andrew was so busy listening that he never heard footsteps coming up behind him. But John had heard them.

HERE HE IS!

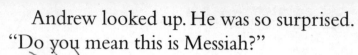

Andrew looked up. He was so surprised.
"Do you mean this is Messiah?"
John nodded.

Andrew jumped up as though he had been stung by a bee. He ran after the man who was walking quickly away from them.

CAN I COME AND TALK WITH YOU?

WHERE DO YOU LIVE?

Messiah smiled. He didn't ask any questions but simply said,

OF COURSE. COME WITH ME.

Andrew spent the rest of the afternoon
talking with Messiah (and doing quite a bit of
listening too!). He could have spent all day
and all night with this man.

The sun was sinking. "I must be going,"
Andrew said with a sigh. Then he had a
thought.

He raced along the lane that led to their house and…

…straight into his brother who was still fast asleep.

Ooops! Sorry, Simon. But you've got to come. There's someone you have to meet. Come on!

"What's the rush?" Simon grumbled.

But Simon had never in all his life seen Andrew so excited.

"OK," he said, scrambling to his feet. "Which way?"

It was dark by the time they got to Messiah's house. The room was lit by an oil lamp.

THIS IS MY BROTHER, SIMON.

He looked closely at Simon and then said a most extraordinary thing.

And for once, Simon didn't argue.

So that's how Simon's name changed.

# CHAPTER 2

# A BAD NIGHT'S FISHING

Jesus was in the middle of a crowd of people trying to walk along the beach. People kept asking him questions, all at once.

He couldn't answer everyone at the same time. The crowd was so big that people at the back and side couldn't hear. They got close to where Peter was sitting mending his nets. He had not caught any fish last night but his nets still needed mending. He was fed up! The crowd nearly fell over his feet and nets.

"Hmmmph!" Peter muttered. In his head, he thought, "You should look where you're going!"

"Peter, could you help me out?" Jesus asked.

Peter looked up, puzzled.

"Can I borrow your boat? Push me out into the lake, just a bit, then everyone can see me and hear what I've got to say."

Peter was pleased Jesus had remembered his new name. Jesus got into the boat. Then Peter waded into the water, pushed the boat out a few metres and climbed in beside Jesus. Andrew was in the boat too.

Jesus' voice carried clearly over the water. Everyone could hear him and the crowd got bigger and bigger.

What Jesus said sounded very important.

Everyone listened. No one talked or coughed or wriggled.

The word 'Peter' is like the Greek word for Rock. Because he was a strong, brave man, Peter was a good choice to be one of the first leaders of the church. Jesus sometimes called him Simon Peter.

So is he called Peter?

Or Simon? ❏     Or Simon Peter?  ❏
Or Rock?  ❏     Or Rock Simon?  ❏
Or Peter Rock? ❏    Aaaarrghhh!!!!  ❏

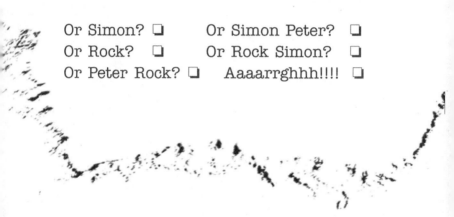

At last Jesus stopped speaking. "Thanks for the loan of the boat," he said to Peter. "Now I'd like to do something for you."

ROW YOUR BOAT INTO THE DEEP WATER, THROW YOUR NETS OVER THE SIDE AND CATCH SOME FISH.

THAT'S DAFT, JESUS. WE WERE FISHING ALL LAST NIGHT AND ONLY CAUGHT BUCKETFULS OF SLIME! IT'S DAYLIGHT NOW. NO FISH WILL BE AROUND HERE!

JESUS IS ONLY A CARPENTER. WHAT DOES HE KNOW ABOUT FISHING?

OK, JESUS. IF THAT'S WHAT YOU WANT ME TO DO.

The brothers rowed into the deep
water. Andrew piled the nets over the
side of the boat. Jesus just sat there.

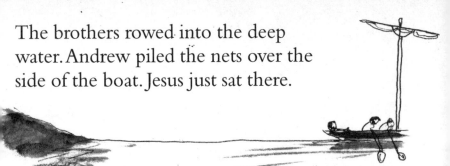

As the nets hit the water, there were flashes
of tiny lights in the water. The sun reflected
off the shiny, wriggling curves of hundreds of
small fishes that had somehow got caught in
the nets! It happened so quickly… before
Peter could blink twice…

James and John came to the rescue. Their boat
quickly filled with fish and looked as though
it would sink. Peter's boat was even worse!
Wriggling fish were everywhere… caught in
Peter's sleeve… mixed up with the
oars and sails… even stuck
in Peter's hair!

Somehow they dragged the nets onto the beach. All five men struggled to tip the two boats upside down to get all the fish out!

Peter no longer felt cross. Instead he felt a big hole inside, much, much bigger than the new holes in his nets. He had thought that Jesus knew nothing about fishing. He had thought that he, Peter, knew more than this man Jesus. He dropped down on his knees.

"I'm not good enough for you, Jesus," he said. "Don't ask me to help you again."

Jesus smiled at Peter and pulled him to his feet. The two of them stood there.

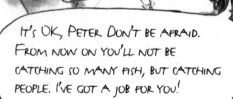

It's OK, Peter. Don't be afraid. From now on you'll not be catching so many fish, but catching people. I've got a job for you!

You need a big net to catch a person. What does Jesus mean?

I think Jesus meant that Peter would find people to bring them to Jesus. And what will Jesus tell them?

Important things, su God wants be his frie

Wow! Peter has got a big job to do!!

30

Peter, Andrew, James, John and Jesus pulled the boats up the beach.

"Come on, all of you," Jesus said. "I'll race you home. Then I'll explain what I want you to do!"

Later, Jesus told Peter and the others that he wanted them to follow him and learn to tell God's message to others.

This message was that God wants us to be his friend.

Phew, it was going to be tough. It was certainly going to be an adventure!

You can read this story in Luke 5:1-11

# CHAPTER 3

# PETER PUTS HIS FOOT IN IT!

Peter loved being with Jesus. He learnt so much about how God wants us to live. He watched how Jesus talked with people and listened to all he said, even though he did not always understand.

One day Jesus talked to a crowd of people on the other side of the lake from where Peter did his fishing.

Jesus didn't seem to hear the question. He helped to push the boat out on to the lake and waved as the wind caught the sails. Peter and his friends would be home very soon if the wind blew like this. Peter still wondered how Jesus would get home. It was a long way to walk round the lake.

The boat sped across the water. The moonlight glittered on the waves. This was a good night for sailing. Peter sighed with happiness.

But suddenly, a cloud
slid across the moon.

The noise in the sails
changed. There was a
storm on the way. Peter
and his friends looked at
each other.

This could be bad
news. The boat was still
moving, but not very fast.

Up and down...
Rolling this way and back...
Round and round...
Water began to slop into the boat. Peter felt sick. "We're in big trouble," he shouted. This was going to be one of the longest and fiercest storms he had ever known!

All night the boat was thrown about on the lake. Peter soon felt tired out – they all did. The wind was so noisy and they were wet through. Just before it began to get light, Peter saw something which made his eyes stand out on stalks!

WWWWWWWHAT'S THAT...?????????

The others turned to see what Peter meant. They all stared.

"It's a ghost!"

Andrew and John screeched together. They all screamed. They screamed so loudly that every gull on the lake could hear them, even above the noise of the wind.

But even louder than that was a voice that they all heard.

WHAT'S THE PROBLEM? IT'S ME, JESUS! DON'T BE SCARED!

Peter leapt up. "Is it you, Jesus? Is it really you? How are you walking on water? Can I come and join you?" He wasn't afraid at all now!

"Yes, come over here, Peter," Jesus said.

This was when Peter really put his foot in it, or 'on it'. He stepped out of the boat, out on to the steep waves and slippery water. It felt cold under his feet but not too cold. It was firm, even though he had to climb up and down the waves. He was walking on water – just doing what Jesus had told him!

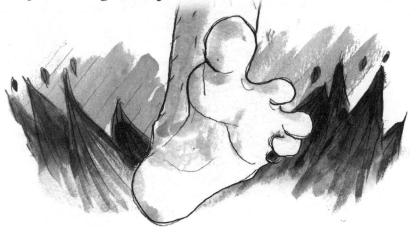

He and Jesus got closer and closer. But then Peter looked down at his feet and…

he suddenly got afraid.  He was going to drown.

Jesus was there, with his arm stretched out. He grabbed hold of Peter, pulled him above the water and they got into the boat.

"Why didn't you trust me, Peter? You would have been OK."

It was then that Peter noticed that
the wind had died down. The storm had
stopped and the boat was almost home.
Everyone was amazed.

Peter never forgot
    the night
his feet
    walked
    on
    water!

You can read
this story in
Matthew 14:22-33

43

# CHAPTER 4
# WASHED FEET

Every now and again Jesus talked about dying soon or having enemies who would get him! Peter got upset by this. He didn't understand!

It was Thursday and Jesus had brought his friends to the big city of Jerusalem. Crowds of people were there. It was the time of year for the important Passover Festival. This was when everyone remembered how God had kept his people safe hundreds of years ago at the time of Moses.

All Jesus' friends met in the evening in an upstairs room to eat the special Passover meal together. This was the best piece of roasted lamb any of them ate in the whole year. Yum!

As usual it had been a hot and sticky day. Peter was tired. He flopped down on the floor expecting a servant to come and wash his dusty feet with cool water.

That was what usually happened. There was always so much dirt on the roads.

But *no one* came to wash *his* feet.

HAVE WE GOT TO SIT ALL THROUGH THE PASSOVER MEAL WITH DIRTY FEET?

LOOKS LIKE IT! MY FEET FEEL HORRIBLE!

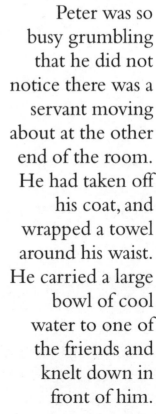

Peter was so busy grumbling that he did not notice there was a servant moving about at the other end of the room. He had taken off his coat, and wrapped a towel around his waist. He carried a large bowl of cool water to one of the friends and knelt down in front of him.

That must feel better! Peter stared as the servant got up, picked up the bowl and moved on to the next person. He couldn't believe his eyes. The servant was Jesus!

Jesus was doing a dirty, smelly job – washing other people's feet! For once, Peter sat in silence, watching Jesus. He was surprised that the other friends let Jesus wash their feet.

At last, Jesus reached Peter. Peter's feet were especially hard with dirt. He curled his feet up underneath him.

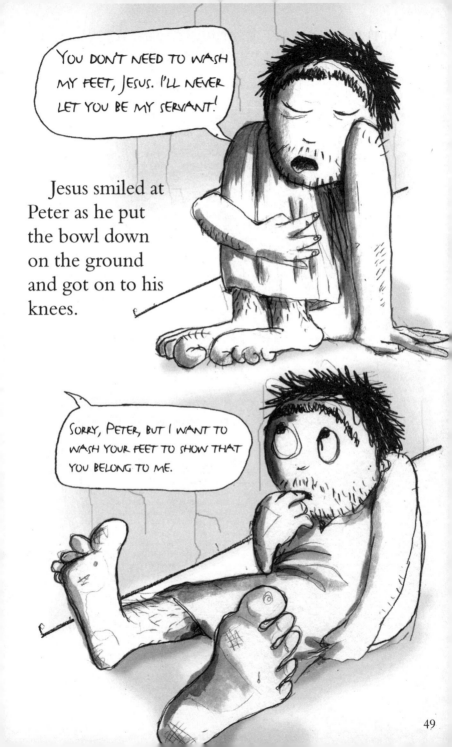

Jesus smiled at Peter as he put the bowl down on the ground and got on to his knees.

49

That shook Peter. "I certainly want to belong to you, Jesus," he said. "So don't stop at my feet..."

He looked around at the others. "You're all more or less clean. You all belong to me, except one of you is still dirty inside."

With that, he washed Peter's smelly feet. "You belong to me, Peter," he said with a sad smile, "and you should all serve each other like this."

51

Peter thought about what it would mean to serve others.

Later that night, Jesus was taken as a prisoner and lots of untrue things were said about him. And all that he had said about getting hurt and dying came true. Jesus went on putting other people before himself. He didn't just wash people's dirty feet.

He died for them.

you can read this story in John 13: 1-20

# CHAPTER 5

# SLOW FEET

Peter was sad – so
sad that he kept
crying. Jesus was
dead! All along Jesus
had warned Peter
this would happen.
Peter had not
believed it was
possible.

Jesus had been taken as a prisoner, put on trial and
then nailed to a cross. Peter had watched him die. His
body was put inside a cave and a stone was rolled over

All day Saturday, Peter remained inside the house where he was staying in Jerusalem.

He felt so empty inside, so lost, so sad. He had spent three years with Jesus, the best years of his life. And now Jesus was gone.

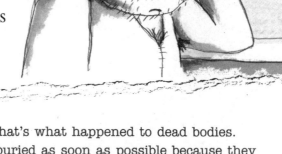

the entrance. (That's what happened to dead bodies. And they were buried as soon as possible because they began to smell.) This happened on a Friday.

Peter woke early the next morning, just after the sun had come up. Birds were singing loudly outside. He rolled onto the floor from his bedmat and sat up. He heard quick footsteps coming down the lane outside.

BANG BANG BANG!

That was the front door!

PETER, LET ME IN! HE'S GONE!

Peter pulled the door open.

WHO'S GONE?
WHERE?

On the doorstep stood Mary Magdalene, one of the women Jesus had helped. She was wide-eyed and out of breath. Just behind her was John.

57

The cave was in a garden which belonged to an important man called Joseph. Peter grabbed his cloak. The two men set off as fast as they could go. But John could run faster than Peter. Peter's feet were too slow!

John called as he turned the corner.

Peter panted.

As he turned the corner, he saw John was already in the garden at the entrance to the cave. Peter saw that the big stone really had been rolled to the side. Peter watched as John stopped and then bent to look inside.

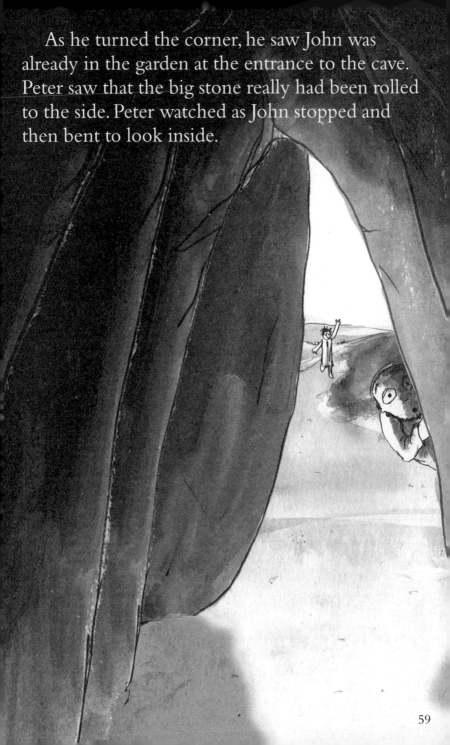

Peter shook his head.

I DON'T BELIEVE WHAT I'M SEEING! WE MUST GO AND TELL THE OTHERS!

The two men were too shocked to speak or run. Where was Jesus?

It was Mary who was to discover the answer to that question. She was crying so loudly that she almost didn't hear footsteps behind her. She thought it was the gardener.

"Have you taken Jesus' body away? If you have, can you tell me where you've put it?"

The gardener simply said,

There was only one
person who said
"Mary" like that. That
was Jesus! Mary
could not believe
what she had seen or
heard. It was Jesus!
He was alive!

She talked with Jesus
for a short time but then
dashed off to tell Peter and
the others that it really was
true!

Jesus really was alive! She had seen him.
And later that day, Jesus met Peter too, along
with the others.

Peter wasn't sad any more. He still didn't understand everything. But he knew that even though he got lots of things wrong, even though he kept putting his foot in it, Jesus was still with him. Jesus was still his friend!

You can read this story in John 20:1-18

Where would his feet take him next?